Trish's Team

Lady Tigers' Series

By

Dawn Brotherton

Trish's Team
Lady Tigers Series

Published by Blue Dragon Publishing

www.blue-dragon-publishing.com

Copyright 2015 Dawn Brotherton

ISBN 978-1-939696-11-3 (ePub)

ISBN 978-1-939696-12-0

Discover other titles by Dawn Brotherton at
http://www.blue-dragon-publishing.com/authors/dawn-brotherton/

Blue Dragon Publishing

Dedication

To the most important people in my life—
Rachel and Paige. Thank you for all you've
taught me. I love you.

And a special thanks to Tori's Reading
Roundtable in Williamsburg, Virginia for
providing their inputs!

Chapter 1

Trish Murphy stood in center field and brushed her brown bangs off her forehead with the back of her right hand. Frowning in concentration, she waited for the next pitch. In front of her, Ashley stepped onto the pitcher's mound, hesitated only briefly, and then spun her right arm in a clockwise motion to deliver a good-looking pitch. *Smack*. The ball sailed toward center field. Racing forward, Trish got under it, just like the coach had shown her. *Plop*. It landed snugly in her glove for an easy out.

"Nice catch, Trish!" Coach Tim called from the dugout. She smiled and threw the ball to the infield. It was a beautiful throw, yet it bounced out of the second baseman's glove and rolled to the pitcher.

Rolling her eyes in frustration, Trish hurried back to her spot in the outfield.

Two outs, one to go.

Trish watched as, on the mound, Ashley took the signal from the catcher. Nodding, Ashley positioned the ball inside her glove, stood tall on her wind up, and fired the ball to the exact low-inside location the catcher had indicated.

"Strike one," the umpire called.

Shifting her stance to the right slightly so she could look around the pitcher's back, Trish waited to see where the next pitch would cross the plate. She was betting it would be low and outside this time.

"Strike two!" she heard across the plush grass that lay before her.

Yep, low and outside, she thought, grinning. Ashley was a pretty good pitcher, and with Alisha catching for her, they were a great team.

Trish knew the next pitch would be a change-up, high and inside. She smiled as the batter was caught off guard, swinging before the ball had even reached the plate. "Strike three! Batter's out!" the ump called.

"Yes!" the team cheered as they raced for the dugout.

Coach Tim met them as they ran off the field, holding his hand out for high-fives. "Come on, girls, gather around. Nice catch out there, Trish. Beautiful strike-outs, Ashley. We're behind by one run. Let's swing some sticks."

The Blue Birds was a recreational fast-pitch softball team for 11- and 12-year-old girls that only played 10 games a summer. The coaches were volunteers and mostly dads of the girls on the team. Trish felt lucky that she was on Coach Tim's team. Some of the dads didn't even know how to play softball, let alone teach the girls to play. Coach Tim was different. He had played baseball in college, so at least he knew the game.

Trish glanced around the softball complex hoping her mom might be there. She didn't really expect to see her, but she was disappointed anyway.

She heard a loud cheer come from the field behind where the Blue Birds were playing. She saw the orange and black uniforms of the Lady Tigers. Trish sighed. She would love to play for the Tigers. The coaches only picked the best-of-the-best players for the travel softball team. They played ball almost every weekend in long tournaments.

"Head in the game, Trish," Coach Tim said, refocusing her attention on her own team.

"Come on, Becky, you can do it!" Trish yelled to the leadoff batter.

Trish turned to read the lineup hanging on the fence. It was the top of the line-up. Trish grabbed her helmet and bat. She was batting fourth.

Hearing the crack of the bat, she looked up in time to see Becky hit a short pop-up to the third baseman. The player tried to catch it, but the ball dropped in front of her, and Becky beat out the throw to first.

"Batter up!" The umpire seemed in a hurry to keep the game moving. Clara quickly stepped inside the chalk-outlined rectangle of the batter's box. The pitch came quickly on the inside corner. "Strike one."

Clara stepped out and took a few practice swings. She settled into the box again. It turned into a long wait as the pitcher threw four balls in a row. Clara jogged to first; Becky went to second.

Trish watched in anticipation as Samantha moved toward home plate for her turn at bat. Trish put on a helmet and stepped out of the dugout to take a few practice swings, getting her timing down for the pitches.

Samantha stepped into the box. She was tall so the outfielders backed up, anticipating that she would hit the ball far. *Crack.* The ball flew over the third baseman's head, landing in the grass. The left fielder raced in and scooped up the ball, preventing the runners from scoring.

Bases loaded. No outs. Trish stepped into the box. She knew she didn't look very impressive. At only four-foot-six, she hadn't reached her full height by a long shot. Her legs were long, slender, and solid muscle. She was used to people underestimating her, but she liked it that way. It usually worked to her advantage.

Trish settled in as the pitcher began her wind up. The pitch came in. Way inside. Trish leaped out of the way. The next pitch was outside, and the catcher missed it. Becky raced past Trish to cross the plate as the fans cheered.

"Just a base hit, Trish," her coach called.

"You can do it, Trish!" The fans were all cheering her on. She kept her concentration on the ball leaving the pitcher's hand.

The pitch was coming in perfect, right down the middle, ideal height. It was slow, so Trish looked at it again. It had a weird spin. She didn't swing. Right before the plate, it dropped. "Ball three." Trish was thankful for the many hours of extra batting practice Coach Tim had spent with her. He had shown her how to truly watch the ball.

The next pitch was almost the same, but it didn't appear to be spinning. *Smack.* It went over the second baseman, missing the right fielder's glove and rolled all the way to the fence for a triple. Clara and Samantha scored as Trish rounded the bases.

The fans were cheering. The score now read, "Blue Birds: 9; Redhawks: 7."

"Nice hit, Trish," Coach Tim said, smiling broadly.

Trish's grin lit up her face. She clapped her hands and cheered on the next batter from third base.

Alisha hit a nice single to left center field that allowed Trish to score. The girls lined up to high-five her as she came into the dugout.

Ashley hit a fly ball to right field that cost them an out, but moved Alisha to third. Amber grounded out on a hit to second base, leaving Alisha in place. Ton-Lou flew out to left field to end the inning. The girls were in high spirits because they were winning, and the other team only had one more chance to bat.

"Good inning, ladies; let's hit the field. Hold them for three more outs," the coach said.

The first Redhawk hit the ball to Lexi on second base who easily picked it up and threw her out at first. Trish was a little nervous when the other team's number four batter stepped to the plate. She was tall for a

12-year-old and had already hit it to the fe
once this game. She took a few steps back
and angled toward left field.

Ashley delivered the pitch low and inside.
The batter got under the ball, and it went high
into foul territory on the left field side. Much
to Trish's surprise, Ashley put the next pitch
in the same place. This time the batter swung
and missed.

Trish smiled. She knew the coaches called
the pitches from the dugout. She would have
to ask Coach Tim why he called two in a row
the same way. That wasn't very common. She
liked to learn as much as she could about the
strategy of softball, not just the technique.

The third and final pitch stayed low but to
the outside corner. The batter swung but
didn't even come close. Two outs.

The number five batter had hit the ball to
center field twice already in previous innings
so Trish was ready. The batter let the first

pitch go by but got ahold of the second. It was a long fly ball to deep center field.

Trish immediately turned her body and began to run toward the fence. She ran full out, praying her left fielder would be there to back her up if she missed it. At the last possible second, Trish dove at where she predicted the ball would be, capturing it in her glove as she hit the ground. That ended the game; final score was 10-7, Blue Birds.

The girls cheered enthusiastically. Trish couldn't stop smiling as the coach and other girls clapped her on the back as they lined up to shake hands with the Redhawks. Even some of the opposing team members congratulated her on such a great catch. It felt wonderful!

She looked around at the crowd waiting outside the fence, but there was no sign of her parents. Trish wished that they had been there to witness her final catch.

Chapter 2

After the game, Trish gathered her equipment. She was walking to the curb when a man about her dad's age approached her. He had a friendly smile and wore a baseball cap over black hair. "Hi, I'm Coach Kory," he said, offering his hand.

Trish took it timidly, but said nothing.

He went on, "I coach for the Lady Tigers fast-pitch softball organization. I saw you play today, and your coach told me that you're a strong ball player."

Her heart started pounding. She couldn't believe Coach Tim had been talking about her to the coach of the Tigers!

"I'd like you to try out for our 12- to 14-year-old team," Coach Kory said, handing her a card. It had Wednesday's date, 5:00 pm, and the name of a ball field that wasn't far from her house written on it.

"Thank you, sir," she replied politely. She wanted to make a good impression. "I'll have to ask my parents."

"Of course. My number's on the back of the card. Tell them they can give me a call any time if they have any questions." He paused. "Do *you* have any questions?" he asked.

Her mind was racing. The Lady Tigers were the big league. They had their banners up all over town. "Where do you travel to?"

Coach Kory smiled. "Most of our games are within an hour of here. It's called travel ball because it's the more competitive league. We only take on the girls who really want to work on getting better."

"Oh, I want to do that!" Trish said before she could stop herself.

"I could tell that about you. You seem to play your heart out. So will I see you at the tryouts?"

"I'll try," Trish said. A flash of sunlight glinting off a windshield caught her eye. "There's my mom. I gotta go. Thank you." Trish waved as she walked to the parking lot, lost in thought about the possibilities of playing travel ball. She really liked playing with the girls on the Blue Birds, but overall the team wasn't very good skill-wise. They had a few talented players, but most were still learning the game. On a competitive team, she would play with girls as good as or better than she was.

She practically floated to her mother's idling car. Her mom had her head buried in a fashion magazine while she waited for Trish to load her gear into the back.

As Trish slid into the backseat, she struggled with whether or not to tell her mother about Coach Kory's offer.

13

When her mother frowned at her through the rearview mirror, taking in her dirty clothes, shoes, hair, and face, Trish decided to keep silent. Her mother preferred to have everything very clean.

"I don't see the point of that silly sport, Patricia," her mother said. "Can't you leave any of that dirt on the court?"

She hated that her mother called her Patricia. It sounded so stuffy. "It's a field, Mother," Trish explained for the millionth time. Her parents never came to her games, so they didn't bother learning the rules or terminology.

"Whatever. It's still silly."

"It's not silly," Trish objected, a little too harshly.

"Don't talk back to me, young lady!"

"Whatever," she muttered under her breath. She crossed her arms in front of her chest and stared out the side window.

Trish had joined the recreational softball team this past spring because a friend from school was playing. As an only child, this gave Trish the chance to play with other kids outside of school. Her coach had said she was a natural, and now she was hooked. But school had just ended and the recreation season was almost over. The Lady Tigers would give her the chance to keep playing.

When they got home, her mother stepped from the car without a word, leaving Trish to unload her gear.

Inside, her father was making himself a snack in the kitchen. "How was the game, honey?" he asked. "Score any runs? You know when I was a kid, I was the quarterback for the best football team in the state. And I was a brilliant QB, not to brag or anything." He grabbed his bowl of chips and soda and headed toward the family room.

Trish sighed and rolled her eyes. She had heard his football stories more times than she cared to count. "Actually, I had a great game. I hit a triple that scored two runs."

Her dad had been distracted by something on the television and didn't hear anything she was saying.

Frustrated, Trish spun on her heels and walked briskly out of the room. Her father earned a substantial income. She knew that he didn't get that way by sitting around, twiddling his thumbs. She just wished he had more time for her. It was lonely being an only child.

"Patricia, wash up, then practice your violin!" her mother called after her.

As she walked to her room, Trish pulled out the band that held her long, light brown hair back in a ponytail. She ran her hands through it to get some of the dirt out. Glancing down at her filthy uniform, she noticed that the pants were already getting too short for her long legs. Her mother said it was another growth spurt and wouldn't even think about getting her new clothes until school started. Seventh grade seemed so far off. Trish wasn't particularly excited about moving up to junior high school.

She stepped into her room. It was decorated with pictures of the best softball players in the world. She started to sit on the bed, but with her dirty clothes, thought better of it. Dropping to the floor to lie flat on her back, Trish stared at the picture of Brittney Parker. She and her younger sister Courtney played in the National Softball League. They were the first sisters to play on the same team. Brittney was the pitcher and Courtney was the catcher. The thought of the Parker sisters always cheered her up. She dreamed of what it would be like to have someone that she loved share her passion for softball.

Trish was thankful for everything she had, but sometimes she wished that she was someone else.

Chapter 3

Trish's bike wobbled slowly to a stop behind the dugout. Her gear was precariously positioned on her handlebars, and any sudden movement would send it flying. She managed to get her feet on the ground and grab the bag before it fell. Climbing off her bike, she let it hit the ground. As she hauled her bag around the dugout, she noticed the girls were already on the field throwing the ball.

It had taken her longer than she planned to get to the field. Her parents were working, and she didn't have a ride, so she had Googled the park and mapped out the best route for her to take, avoiding any busy roads. She wasn't allowed to ride her bike outside her neighborhood, but she didn't think her parents would notice, as long as she was home before they were, and that shouldn't be too hard.

Quickly unzipping her bag, she grabbed her glove and ran onto the field.

Coach Kory waved at her as she approached.

"I'm sorry I'm late," she said, breathing hard from rushing.

"Don't worry about it," he said. "You haven't missed anything. Grab a ball and find someone to play catch with."

Trish got a ball from the bucket he indicated and headed to the end of the line. Three girls were throwing together, and one of them broke off to throw with her.

She started her throws off easy, the way she had been taught. As she warmed up, her throws became harder and harder. She focused on her accuracy. She loved the feel of just throwing the ball, not a care in the world.

That's why she liked softball so much. She could lose herself in the game.

Trish jumped for a particularly high throw and snagged it in the web of her glove.

"Nice catch!" the girl standing next to her said.

"Thanks," Trish grinned back at her.

"I'm Nikki. That's my sister Sally," the girl said gesturing to her throwing partner, "but she'd rather be called Sal."

Sal waved at Trish.

Trish took in their height, dark hair and coffee-colored skin and asked, "Are you twins?"

The sisters laughed as they continued to play catch. "Everyone asks us that," Nikki explained. "That's why Sal finally cut her hair—to look different from me, but it hasn't helped." Nikki's long hair was as dark as Sally's, but was held back in a braid.

"I'm a year older and wiser," Sal said.

"Not sure anyone would consider a 13-year-old wise," Nikki teased her.

Trish looked down the line of girls that had come to the tryout. Her eyes fell on a thin girl at the end of the row. Her glove was clearly too small, and she was having a hard time catching anything. Two of the girls near her snickered when she dropped the ball for the third time.

It was obviously from the look on Nikki's face that she had noticed the girls that were being mean too. "I don't know why some people have to act like that," Nikki said.

Sal's eyes followed her sister's gaze and nodded in agreement.

"It's really not her fault," Trish said. "I think the girl she's playing catch with is trying to make her miss."

The girls were interrupted by the pitching coach calling for all pitchers and catchers to join him at the backstop. Trish watched as

Nikki jogged over to the disheartened girl. "What's your name?" Nikki asked.

"Margie Clark." The girl was so downtrodden that she didn't even lift her head to meet Nikki's eyes.

"I'm Nikki. Don't sweat this stuff," Nikki said. "It's early and you have plenty of time." She held out her glove, "Try this. I'll be using my catcher's mitt for a while so I won't need it. I think your glove is just too small."

Margie accepted the offered gift and lifted her face with a smile. "Thanks."

"No problem," Nikki said, jogging off to meet the others.

Trish smiled to herself. These were the kind of girls she wanted to hang out with.

She focused on Coach Kory as he talked to the remaining fielders about the outfield drill they were going to run. "Line up at center field. I'll hit you a fly ball. Catch it and hit your cutoff." He selected a girl to be the cutoff, telling her to stand midway between the outfielder and the catcher to make the throws shorter.

Trish smiled as Margie made a nice catch in center field and fired it to the cutoff person. Her smile broadened when the next girl missed a fly ball that was catchable. She was one of the girls who had been making fun of Margie during warm-ups.

Twenty minutes later, Coach Kory waved the girls in and called to get everyone's attention.

"Okay, girls. Drop your gloves and line up at home plate," Coach Kory said.

The girls all discarded their equipment and jogged to the backstop.

"First, I want you all to jog out to the right field fence and back to loosen your legs. This is not a race. Take your time and warm up your muscles. Go on," he gestured to the outfield.

Trish noted the girls that took off at a full run at the word *go*. She shook her head in dismissal at their foolishness and continued her comfortable pace. Nikki ran at her side.

"Thanks for letting me use your glove," Margie said, jogging up beside Nikki. "You're right. I think my glove's too small."

"No worries. Margie, this is Trish," Nikki said. She pointed to Sal running on the other side of Trish. "And that's my sister Sal—no, we aren't twins," she added before Margie had a chance to ask.

Sally gave a little wave, but didn't speak as she jogged along. The girls touched the right field fence and headed back. They arrived at home plate with the majority of the girls; only three had pushed ahead to ensure they were first.

"You four go with Coach Dave," Coach Kory said randomly pointing at a group of girls. "You four go with Coach Sam, and the rest of you stay with me."

The girls split up and went with their coaches to various areas along the third base line.

One at a time, the girls ran the length of the baseline while the coaches timed them and jotted down their results. They each got three attempts to show their speed before the coaches sent them running laps around the outside of the fence surrounding the field.

After two full laps, the coaches sent them to the dugout for water.

The next drills were standard infield grounders hit by the coach. The girls took turns scooping them up and throwing the ball to first base. The coaches rotated them through all positions in the infield, including pitcher and catcher.

"Nikki, get your catcher's gear on. Sal, on the mound," Coach Kory called out. One by one, he placed the girls in a position on the field.

Trish was disappointed that she was placed at second base. She knew her strength was in the outfield where she could run full-out. She felt her strong arm was wasted with the short throw from second base to first, and she was worried she wasn't showing the coaches her best plays. She held her feelings in check, though, and would do her best to field the ball as the girls took turns batting.

Sally stepped up to the mound. She threw five warm-up pitches, then the first batter stepped into the box. It was simple; the batter struck out, one, two, three. The next batter fouled off a few pitches before also striking out. The third batter didn't have any luck either.

When it was Trish's turn to get in the batter's box, she felt the sweat dripping down her face. It was her shot against Sal. The last batter had struck out without so much as getting the bat on the ball. Trish was a good hitter, but Sal was a better pitcher than she was used to.

The first pitch was quick on the low, inside corner. Trish swung and was way late. She cringed at the sound of the ball hitting the catcher's mitt.

"C'mon, Trish, you can do it!" Margie yelled from left field.

Trish smiled her appreciation before stepping back into the box.

Sally bent down and ran her fingers through the dirt. She stood and wiped her hand on her pants before stepping back onto the rubber.

"You and me, Sal," Nikki called from behind the plate. "Like always."

Trish was hanging back off the plate so she guessed Nikki would call for a pitch high and outside.

As Sally started her wind up, Trish moved closer to the plate. It was too late for the pitcher to adjust. Trish timed it perfectly and connected with the ball, driving it into right field.

Nikki stood up and removed her mask. She patted Trish on the shoulder, "That was a great move. How'd you read her?"

Trish shrugged. "It's what I would've called if I were catching."

Nikki laughed. "Do you catch, too?"

"Nah. I like center field better, but I watch the catcher's signs, so I know where to stand."

"Very smart," Nikki acknowledged.

The ball had been returned to the pitcher, so Nikki put her mask back on and crouched behind the plate.

After all the girls got their turn at bat, Coach Kory called them together in the pitcher's circle. "Girls, this has been a great first tryout. I'm excited that so many of you took time out of your day to be here. As you know, I only have a few slots opening up this season, so I can't pick all of you, although I'd love to! You're a great bunch of kids." The other coaches tossed in their agreements.

"There will be at least two more tryouts scheduled in the next two weeks. You're more than welcome to come to all of them, or just this one. That's up to you."

Trish knew anyone who didn't come to all the tryouts was probably doomed. Their lack of dedication would come out. She wasn't about to make that mistake. She hoped the other tryouts wouldn't be on Wednesdays when she had orchestra practice.

She still didn't know what her parents would think if she made the team, but she would worry about that later. *One thing at a time*, she thought. No sense bringing it up if she wasn't going to make it anyway.

"So, the next tryout is Sunday afternoon at 2:00, right here on this field. Plan on another two hours at least," Coach Kory said. "Let's bring it in."

The girls circled around and placed their right hand into the center. "Softball on the count of three," he said. "One, two, three..."

"Softball!" they all yelled in unison, throwing their hands into the air.

Trish concentrated on balancing her softball bag on her handlebars. She was hot and sweaty but felt very good about the practice.

"Great job today!" Sally said, walking up to Trish.

"You, too! What an arm!"

"Thanks. Nikki and I have spent many long days throwing the ball around in the backyard."

Trish was envious. She wished she had someone to throw with.

"What about you? Do you have brothers and sisters?" Sally asked.

"No such luck. It's just me, and my parents think you score touchdowns in softball."

Sally laughed. Nikki walked up to them and let her gear drop. "What's so funny?"

"Parents!" Sally answered.

"Oh! Were you telling her about how Mom and Dad embarrass us by holding up signs in the bleachers? And try to get the wave started?"

"Ouch!" Trish said.

"Yeah, we try to pretend we don't know them, but they do feed us," Nikki said.

"Speaking of which," Sally nudged her sister and pointed at the minivan pulling into the parking lot.

"See you Sunday?" Nikki asked Trish.

"Of course! See you then!"

The girls waved as they headed toward the van.

Trish wrapped the straps of her bag around the handlebars and carefully climbed on her bike. With a push of her right foot, she set off for home.

Chapter 4

Trish walked with Margie to the parking lot where Mrs. Clark was waiting for Margie.

"How was practice, honey?" Margie's mom asked as her daughter approached the open window.

Her sister, Tara, squealed in delight to see her big sister. Margie leaned in the back window and poked her in the belly, making her laugh.

"It started out horrible! Mom, can I get a new glove *please*? Mine's too small."

Her mother smiled at her sympathetically.

"But I did meet the greatest people," Margie said excitedly. She waved Trish closer. "Mom, this is Trish."

"Nice to meet you," Trish said.

"It's nice to meet you too, Trish. I'm glad you two made friends."

Margie continued talking as she loaded her gear into the back of the car. "And there are two other girls—they're sisters! Nikki is a catcher and her sister Sal is a pitcher. They're a great team! I couldn't catch a thing during warmups, then Nikki let me borrow her glove."

"So you made lots of friends. That's good."

Margie nodded. "The girls were great. Well, most of them anyway. Some were kind of snotty."

"But you could out run them!" Trish added.

"You're really fast too, especially in the outfield. I'll bet you make the team," Margie said.

"How do you think you did?" Mrs. Clark ask Margie.

"Not bad after I started using Nikki's glove. And Trish showed me a few tricks about how to stand in the outfield to get a better start when the ball's hit."

"Sounds like a great first day!" Mrs. Clark said.

"I need to come to all the tryouts, though, if I really want to make the team."

"Well, get in. Let's go get you that glove," her mom said. "Trish, do you need a ride?"

"No, thanks," Trish answered. "I have my bike." She gestured to where she had left her bike behind the dugout.

Margie got into the car, waving to Trish. "See you Sunday."

Margie handed her old glove to Tara, "Here you go. When your hands get big enough, you can have this one."

Tara cooed happily and put one of the cowhide strings in her mouth, sucking the dirt off.

Sunday after church, Trish dressed in shorts and shoved her softball pants into her bat bag. She'd find a place to change when she got to the field.

"Mom, I'm going to Lexi's for a while."

"Did you practice your violin?"

"Yes, ma'am."

"Be home before dinner. Your dad will be back from golfing by then."

"Okay." Trish couldn't remember a Sunday when her dad didn't play golf, even if she had a ball game.

Once again, Trish struggled to balance her gear on her handlebars, and off she went. She rode to Lexi's house a block away, and then kept on going. This time she was one of the first ones to arrive at the field.

"Nice to see you again, Trish," Coach Kory said.

"Hi!" She tried not to drop everything in front of him. "Is there a place I can change?"

"The restrooms are behind the other dugout," he said pointing.

Trish hustled away.

When she ran onto the field, Nikki and Sal were already playing catch. They waved her over and included her in their warmup throws.

"Hi, Margie!" Trish called as Margie jogged up to them. "Grab a ball."

Margie stopped at the bucket and picked up another ball. She threw it to Trish and took her place in line next to Sally.

"Hey, you got a new glove!" Nikki said.

Margie beamed. "Cool, huh? I've been oiling it for days. It fits much better. Thanks for the advice."

The girls fell into a comfortable chatter as other girls joined in, throwing the ball back and forth. Trish noticed that the snotty girls that had laughed at Margie last practice hadn't bothered showing up. They probably figured they were a shoe-in. There were a number of different girls this time. She was really glad she had come to the second tryout.

After ten minutes or so, Coach Kory called them all together, introducing himself and his assistant coaches again for the sake of the new girls. Then he picked one of the girls that had been at the last tryout to lead the stretches.

The third tryout went about the same as the first two. Before the girls knew it, the tryouts were over and Coach Kory was talking about how they would be notified if they were invited to play for the Lady Tigers.

"First I want to thank you all for taking time out of your schedules to be here. And thanks to the parents for sharing your girls with the Lady Tigers." He nodded to the parents.

"As I said at the beginning, we only have a few openings for this year's team. All of you have done great. Whether or not you make the team, don't stop playing. Your talent caught our attention. Keep working and, even if you aren't selected this year, you may want to try out again next summer."

The girls shifted nervously. They knew that the competition was tough and that some of these girls wouldn't be coming to the next practice.

"You'll be getting letters in the mail, one way or the other. Thanks again for playing ball." And with that, Coach Kory shook each of the girls' hands as they gathered their things to leave.

As Trish walked to her bike, Nikki ran over carrying something. "Hey, Trish, want to try this?" She held up a canvas backpack. "It's old, but it would be a lot easier to carry on your bike."

Trish took the offered gift. "Thanks! This is great. But don't you need it?"

"We got new ones for Christmas. It was in the garage. Look, there's even a place to put your bat." She helped Trish transfer her gear from her old gym bag into the backpack.

"This is perfect!" Trish exclaimed, slipping it over her shoulder. "Thanks a million!"

"No problem. See you around!"

Trish was beaming as she hooked the empty bag onto her bike. This was going to be so much easier to ride.

Before she had a chance to take off, Coach Kory called to her, "Trish? I haven't had a chance to meet your parents yet. Do you think they'll come to the next practice?"

"Um, I'm not sure," Trish said looking at the ground. "They're pretty busy."

"Well, they have to officially sign you up and fill out the forms if you are going to play for the Tigers."

She looked up quickly. "Does that mean I made the team?" she asked hopefully.

"I think there's a good chance, if your parents agree. Can you ask them to give me a call? Do you still have my card?"

"I do." Trish was trying to figure out how she was going to explain this to her parents. "I'll have them call you."

"Great! I look forward to it. Be safe!" He waved and walked up to Margie and her mother as Margie was loading her gear into the car.

Chapter 5

Trish grabbed the mail from the box and flipped through it as she walked up the driveway. She dropped the store flyers and junk mail in the recycle bin next to the kitchen door. She froze in her tracks as she saw a letter addressed to her from Coach Kory.

Trish, I'm glad you decided to try out for the Tigers. You have a lot of talent, but it also takes dedication and hard work to play travel ball.

I would be honored to have you on my team. Please have your parents fill out the enclosed documentation and bring it to the next practice.

Plan on practicing every Saturday and Wednesday for the next few weeks. Our first tournament is in August, and we have a lot of work to do between now and then.

Coach Kory Kerrington

Trish could hardly believe it. She had made the Tigers! Her smile was so broad, she thought it might split her face.

"Patricia? Is that you?" she heard her mother call from the living room.

Her face fell almost as quickly as it had lit up. How was she going to tell her parents? What was she going to tell them? She hadn't even told them she was trying out. Now she needed to break it to them that she was going to have practice every Wednesday night. That was the same night as orchestra rehearsal. She was sure her parents were going to flip.

She tucked the letter into her back pocket and went into the living room to find her mother.

Trish's first call after receiving Coach Kory's letter had been to Margie. Now they were sitting at the frozen yogurt shop waiting for Sally and Nikki to show up to celebrate.

"What do you mean you haven't told your parents?" Margie said in shock. "Where do they think you've been during tryouts?"

Margie's parents looked up at the sound of their daughter's raised voice. They were sitting at the other end of the shop with baby Tara, giving the girls their privacy but keeping an eye on them at the same time. Margie smiled and waved to them that everything was all right.

Trish had the decency to look ashamed. "At my friend's," she answered. "But it's not like they were really paying attention anyway."

"That's not the point!" Margie said. "Won't they be mad when they find out?"

"I don't know," Trish said, running her hands over her face.

The bell on the door jingled and the two girls looked up to see Sally and Nikki come running in. Margie's parents stood up and waved to the newcomers' parents as they followed the girls through the door. The grownups shook hands with the other girls' parents and sat down, instantly engaged in their own conversation.

Trish and Margie postponed their discussion while they waited for Sally and Nikki to get their frozen yogurt and select the toppings.

When they had all sat down, Margie began, "You aren't going to believe this…"

She filled the sisters in on Trish's dilemma.

"Dang! What are you going to do?" Sally asked.

"Just because they don't know much about softball doesn't mean they won't let you play, does it?" Nikki asked.

"No, I don't think so. They let me play rec ball. The problem is practices are on Wednesday night."

"So?" Margie asked.

"I have orchestra on Wednesdays."

"Cool!" Nikki and Sally said together.

All the girls smiled at the unified response.

Nikki asked, "What instrument do you play?"

"Violin," Trish answered.

"I've always wanted to play an instrument," Margie said. "Mom says we can't afford it right now."

"Bummer," Sally said.

Margie shrugged it off. "It's not like we're poor or anything, but an instrument is expensive, and then there's lessons and everything else."

"I don't mind playing," Trish said, "but I'd rather play softball."

"Well, maybe your parents will let you take a few months off," Nikki offered.

"Or maybe you can be in a different orchestra!" Margie suggested. "There's got to be more than one."

It felt good to be talking about this with her friends. They had only met each other a few times, but already Trish knew that she didn't want to give them up.

"Mom?"

"Yes, Patricia?" her mom handed Trish a spoon to stir the broth simmering on the stove.

"There's going to be a lot more homework in junior high."

"Nothing you can't handle," she replied, adding a dash of salt to the pot.

"But it will take up more time."

Her mother placed her finger on the step in the recipe she was following. "Are you getting nervous, Patricia? It's only July."

"No, I'm not nervous," Trish answered honestly. "I'm trying to think ahead. Consider my schedule and everything."

"That's a good idea. I like to see you making plans." She went back to reading her cookbook.

"You know," Trish went on, "music practice takes a lot of time. Every night plus lessons and orchestra."

"Honey, you love orchestra!"

"I do like it," Trish admitted. "It's just that there are so many other things I want to do that I don't have time for."

"Like what?"

"Hang with my friends, read books, family time…"

Her mother laughed and ran her hand down the back of Trish's head. "Sweetheart, you have time for all that."

"Well, right now I do, but when school starts, I'll have lots more homework. And the bus ride is longer, and I may want to join some clubs and stuff."

"Why don't we worry about that when school starts again?" her mother suggested.

"But I don't think you should waste your money on lessons when I'm going to quit in the fall."

"Don't be silly. You aren't going to quit. You've spent years playing violin. You have a chance at a college scholarship at the rate you're going. That's what Professor Matthews said. And we are so proud of you!" Her mom put her arms around Trish and hugged her.

Trish hugged her back with a little less enthusiasm.

Chapter 6

"Trish!" Margie called out when her friend pulled up on her bike on Saturday morning.

Trish waved back and jumped off her bike in one fluid motion. She ran to the dugout to drop her bag. She grabbed her glove and ran to meet her friends. This was the first practice since the entire team was selected, and she was glad to see the girls who had made it.

Nikki was standing next to her as they warmed up throwing the ball. "Did you talk to your parents?"

Trish glanced around but the coaches were still near the dugout and not within hearing distance.

"I tried."

"And what did they say?" Sally joined in.

"Mom is so proud of my music. She thinks I can get a scholarship."

"That's good news, isn't it?" Margie asked. "Are you that good?"

Trish stuck her tongue out at her. "Don't act so surprised. Yeah, I'm pretty good, but I don't like it that much. Not as much as softball."

"I get that," Sally offered. "Don't your parents understand? I think our folks know we live and breathe softball."

"My mom never played sports and doesn't even understand why a girl would want to sweat."

The girls laughed.

"What about your dad?" Margie asked.

Trish thought a moment. "Dad understands football and golf, but that's about it for sports. And girls don't play football. Aside from that, he's only interested in making money. Not a lot of money to be made from softball."

"You could get a scholarship," Sally offered.

"The Parker sisters make money playing for the National Softball League," Nikki said.

"I'm not that good," Trish said. "I just like to play."

"You might not be that good now," Margie said, "but playing on this team can get you there. That's what I'm hoping. I'm going to need a scholarship to get to college. Dad's in the Air Force, and he says he isn't there because it pays well."

"Tigers, line up behind the plate," Coach Kory yelled from the dugout.

At the end of practice, Coach Kory called Trish over. "Your parents never called me. Did you bring the paperwork I asked them to sign?" he asked.

"Sorry, I forgot all about it. We've been so busy, and my folks work late."

"I hear you, Trish, but without that paperwork, you can't play or practice

51

anymore. It's the club rules. It's for insurance purposes.'

"Yes, Coach," Trish said, not meeting his eyes.

"See you Wednesday!" he patted her shoulder and walked away.

Margie joined her as she packed her bat bag. "Are you going to be able to make it Wednesday?"

"This Wednesday I will. Professor Matthews is on vacation, so orchestra was cancelled."

"Then what will you do?"

"I need to figure something out."

"Good luck!" Margie said. Mrs. Clark's car pulled into the lot, and Margie jogged off to meet it.

"Trish, do you have that paperwork for me?" Coach Kory asked when she arrived at practice on Wednesday night.

"Oh, I forgot it," Trish lied. "It's sitting on the kitchen counter." She got off her bike. "I'll bring it Saturday."

"No practice for you today then," Coach Kory said. "I was serious. No paperwork, no practice."

"But, Coach!"

"No buts. I'm strict on rules. That's something you need to learn about me from the beginning."

"Yes, Coach."

"If you hurry, maybe you can ride home and back again before it gets too late."

"Okay." Trish turned her bicycle around and wearily climbed on. As she pedaled slowly home, she dreaded the decision she needed to make. She still hadn't told her parents and they hadn't signed anything. Now she had lied to her coach and she still didn't know what to do. She knew she would have to miss practice.

The next night at dinner, Trish decided to broach the subject with her parents. "Mom, you know those girls I went for yogurt with?"

"Yes, dear. Did you have enough money?" her mom asked as she passed the salad bowl to her husband.

"Sure. Thanks. Well, they play on a softball team."

"That's nice, honey," her father said distractedly. "Please pass the butter."

Trish passed the tub to her father. "They want me to play with them."

"But you're already on a team," her mother said.

"The rec season is over, and besides, this is a really *good* team. The coach only takes the best! And they get to play against top teams in the area. They spend the entire weekend playing tournaments!"

"Sounds dreadful!" her mother said with a shudder.

"Mom! I'm serious. This is a great opportunity!"

"And I suppose you want to play?" her father asked, finally taking an interest.

"Yes!" Trish couldn't believe this was going so well.

"It won't be every weekend, will it?" her mother asked.

"No, of course not. Just a few in the fall and then again in the spring."

"That's it?" her father asked.

"Well, we have to practice, of course."

"And when would that be?"

"Saturday mornings and Wednesday nights," Trish said quietly.

"Then that's not going to work, is it?" her father said, forking food into his mouth. "You already have a commitment on Wednesday nights."

"But I'm really good!" Trish whined. "And I'll get even better playing with these girls! They're great! And a lot of fun."

"Honey," her mother tried to sooth, "I'm glad you've made more friends and maybe you can go watch some of their games, but we've invested a lot in your music. You've played for years. There's no sense throwing that all away now."

"But—" Trish started.

Her father interrupted her, "No more buts. Your mother said you're going to play violin. Let's talk about something else."

Trish knew better than to continue the argument.

After dinner, Trish trudged up the stairs to her room. She glared at the offending violin case that leaned against the wall in the corner. She never even wanted to play violin, but her parents made her. They felt it was good for her. Now it was standing between her and softball, and she resented it even more.

She threw herself down on her bed and contemplated her next move.

On Friday, Trish closed the mailbox and sifted through the mail as she walked up the driveway. She saw the letter from the school and the stack of papers that her parents were required to sign for her junior high classes.

Then a plan began to form in her mind. She practically flew to the house in her excitement. There may be a way for her to get her permission slip signed for Coach Kory after all.

That night after dinner, she finished cleaning the dishes while her mom went to take a shower. Her father made himself a drink and settled in front of the television with his laptop. Trish waited until her father was absorbed in his typing, while at the same time, tuned to the news for any piece of information that might be useful to him.

"Dad?"

"Hmmm?" he answered distractedly.

"I don't mean to bother you, but I have some papers I need you to sign," Trish said.

He didn't even look away from his keyboard. "What for?"

"The school sent some stuff about classes and clubs. Nothing terribly interesting." She slipped the pages in front of him and held out a pen. "You can sign them and I'll put them back in the mail."

He took the pages and scribbled his name quickly on the lines Trish pointed out to him. "That's very responsible of you," he said absently, his focus on the breaking news on the television.

Trish almost snatched the papers from his hands, but made herself stay calm until he handed them back to her. "Thanks, Dad." She ran to her room before he had a chance to ask any questions. She was giddy with relief and fell onto her bed, hugging the pages to her chest.

Chapter 7

When she pedaled to practice the next morning, she was still light-hearted. She had dropped the signed letters in the mail back to the school, just as she had told her dad she would.

"Good morning," Coach Kory said as she jumped off her bike. "You're all smiles this morning!"

"I'm happy to be here!" Trish said. She reached into her backpack and pulled out a few rumpled sheets of paper. She smoothed them ineffectually against her stomach and handed them to the coach. "Sorry this took me so long," she said.

"No problem. I'm just glad you got them turned in. I'd hate to lose you so soon." He smiled and waved her toward the field. "Get out there and warm up!"

Trish grabbed her gear and ran into the outfield to meet her friends.

"Yea! You made it!" cried Margie.

"Your parents signed the permission form?" Sally asked.

"Dad did last night," Trish answered truthfully.

"What about orchestra?" Nikki interjected.

Trish hesitated. She hadn't thought that part through. "We haven't decided yet," she hedged.

"Make a circle!" Coach Dave called out.

Saved by the coach, Trish thought.

As Wednesday drew closer, Trish became more and more anxious. She hadn't figured out how she was going to keep missing orchestra and not get caught. And there was the matter of leaving the house with her violin and her softball gear at the same time.

Wednesday morning her mother was in the kitchen when Trish dragged herself down for breakfast. She was feeling a little queasy, but didn't think she was really getting ill.

"Oh, good. I'm glad you're awake, Patricia. Mrs. Carpenter called this morning and wants to have a meeting tonight for a charity fundraiser. Your dad will be working late. Do you think you could get a ride to orchestra?"

Instantly Trish perked up. "Of course. Not a problem."

Her mom looked at her thoughtfully, "I suppose I can call Abby's mother. She said she wouldn't mind giving you a ride—"

"No really, Mom, I got this. I can find my own ride. Don't worry about it." Trish grabbed an apple out of the fridge. "I'm going to…," Trish stumbled, trying to think of what to say, "um, go practice for a while," she finally managed and dashed out of the kitchen.

Back in her room, she closed the door and sat cross-legged on her bed. She took a bite of her apple and thought about how lucky she was. She wasn't sure how long her luck would hold out, though. She'd have to come up with something fast.

She finished her apple, got up, and washed her hands. Back in her room, she opened the violin case and looked at the beautiful instrument. Picking it up, she ran the bow across the strings a few times to warm up, then sat down in front of her music stand.

As she played the instrument, she got lost in the music. The piece they were working on was challenging, but so much fun. It was lively, then sad, then ended on a happy note—literally. When she finished, she looked up to see her mother standing in the doorway.

"Marvelous, honey. You sound great!" Her mom smiled and walked away.

Trish's stomach started to churn again.

Trish jumped every time the phone rang, afraid it would be her orchestra leader calling her parents about the missed practice. Her luck held, though, and she made it through the week.

Margie came over Friday night and they spent an hour tossing the ball. They threw each other popups, and Trish showed Margie what Coach Tim had taught her about positioning her body for the throw. They laughed and told stories. Although they went to different schools, the antics were the same, and one story led to another.

Before she realized the time, Trish's mom's car was pulling in the driveway.

"Hi, girls!" her mom called as she got out of the car. "Patricia didn't tell me she was having company," she added with a meaningful glance at her daughter.

Trish was smart enough to look shamefaced. It wasn't that she couldn't have friends over. She was just supposed to ask permission first.

"Mom, this is Margie."

"Hi, Margie. Nice to meet you."

"You, too, Mrs. Murphy." She waved with her gloved hand. "You have a lovely home."

"Thank you, dear. Are you staying for dinner? You are more than welcome."

Before Margie could answer, Trish cut in, "Her mom's coming to get her soon. Maybe we'll just get a snack."

Margie looked hurt at Trish's quick dismissal, but she went along with it. "As a matter of fact, I should probably give her a call," she said.

"Maybe next time," Mrs. Murphy said as she went inside. "Patricia, clean up before dinner."

"Yes, ma'am," she mumbled, but her eyes were on Margie.

"Margie, no offense—"

"None taken, Trish. Why would you want someone like me eating at your table?" The sourness in her voice was agonizing. Picking up the ball, she walked to where she had left her cell phone.

Trish looked horrified. "No! It isn't like that at all! It's just...," she didn't want to admit that she had lied, but nothing could be worse than hurting her friend's feelings. "I haven't exactly told my parents about the Tigers yet," she mumbled.

"What?!" Margie yelped. "You said your dad signed the paperwork!"

"He did, technically. He wasn't really paying attention and didn't read what he was signing."

Margie looked sadly at her friend. "This isn't going to end well, you know."

Trish slumped down on the front stoop. "I know. But I want to play so badly! They'll never understand."

"Have you given them the chance?"

"I tried. All they can talk about is music. It's like sports are a bad thing."

Margie sat down beside her friend. "You know they're going to find out."

Trish picked a stone off the pavers and threw it into the bushes. "I know."

"It would be best if they found out from you," Margie added logically.

Sighing, Trish crossed her arms across her knees and buried her face.

Chapter 8

Trish woke up to the patter of rain on the roof. Her first thought was disappointment that practice for that evening would be cancelled. Then she sat bolt upright in bed. Practice would be cancelled! The relief hit her, and she laid back down, cuddling up under the covers.

She hadn't slept well, trying to come up with an excuse not to go to orchestra. Now she didn't have to, and she rested peacefully.

When she finally drug herself out of bed and got dressed, she finished her chores without being reminded. She even cleaned out her closet, packing clothes that were too small for her into a box to be given away.

"Patricia, it looks great in here. What has gotten into you?" her mother asked, taking in the room.

"Just thought I'd take advantage of the weather," Trish replied honestly.

"Well, it's time for lunch. Wash your hands and come down. Maybe we can go shopping this afternoon before orchestra practice."

Trish glanced at the clock. She hadn't realized how late it was. She had been occupied all morning.

"I'll be down in a minute," she told her mom. "I'm almost done in here."

Her mom smiled, saying, "You really surprise me sometimes."

Trish smiled back, but inside, her stomach turned sour. She wasn't sure what her mom would say when she found out about the Lady Tigers. Trish felt lucky to have found such great friends and she didn't want to do anything to mess that up.

After lunch, Trish followed her mom to a variety of clothes stores while her mother shopped.

"What about this one, Patricia?" her mother said, holding up another in a series of shirts against Trish.

"It's fine," Trish replied automatically. She really didn't like clothes shopping and didn't have the same taste in clothes as her mother, but she didn't want to cause a fight.

"Now I know something is wrong," her mother said, catching Trish's attention. "This blouse is ugly and has ruffles. You would never wear it!" She smiled at her daughter, "What's going on?"

Trish forced a smile in return, feeling guilty that she had been caught. She shrugged. "Nothing. Just thinking about things."

Her mother replaced the blouse on the rack. "Well, we're wasting our time here. Let's get you to orchestra practice."

Trish followed her out of the store, disappointed that her mother hadn't tried a little harder to get her to open up. Trish wanted to talk to her mom. She wanted to tell her about all the friends she had made and how much it meant to her to play with the Lady Tigers. But she didn't think her mother would really understand or care.

She was still sullen when her mom dropped her off.

"Trish, we missed you last week. Is everything okay?" the instructor asked her as Trish tuned her violin.

"Ah, yes, it's fine," she stammered, not looking up at him.

"You need to let me know if you won't be here," Professor Matthews reminded her. "We're counting on you."

"Yes, sir," Trish replied. The sick feeling in her stomach returned.

The next evening, Trish went to Margie's house.

"I don't know what I'm going to do," Trish said. "I don't want to let Professor Matthews down, but I also don't want to let our team down." She plopped down on Margie's bed.

"It would have been easier if you hadn't lied to begin with," Margie said.

Trish groaned, covering her face with her hands.

"Girls, come eat," Mrs. Clark called up the stairs.

"Come on," Margie said, grabbing Trish's wrists and pulling her upright. "Mom makes the best comfort food anywhere!"

Trish followed Margie to the kitchen where Mrs. Clark was feeding Tara in her highchair.

The girls took their places.

"Where's Dad?" Margie asked.

"He has to work late," her mother answered, still spooning food into Tara's open mouth. "He said to start without him."

Trish dug into her food. Between mouthfuls she said, "Thanks, Mrs. Clark. This chicken is wonderful!"

Mrs. Clark smiled. "I'm glad you like it." She turned to her daughter, "What's wrong, Margie? I thought chicken alfredo was your favorite?"

Margie shrugged. "Nothing. I'm just thinking." She ran her fork through her noodles, contemplating her question.

"Mom, what would you say if I told you I didn't want to do something anymore that you really wanted me to do?"

Trish's jaw fell open in surprise. *Was Margie going to rat her out?*

Mrs. Clark paused from scooping food into Margie's baby sister's mouth and looked at her. "Like what?"

"I don't know. Does it matter?"

"Sure. If it's homework or chores, you don't have a choice." She resumed her feeding.

Margie giggled. "Not like that. I mean something like art or softball."

Trish kicked Margie under the table. Margie moved her legs out of striking distance.

"Did something happen at softball? I thought you had made a lot of friends there." Mrs. Clark glanced meaningfully at Trish.

"Everything's good," she assured her mother. "It's just..."

Her mom wiped off Tara's mouth and removed the bib. She picked her up from the highchair and set her carefully on the floor. Tara dropped to her knees and quickly headed for the living room and the toys she had left on the carpet.

"Margie, why don't we go take care of Tara so your mom can eat?" Trish suggested helpfully, trying to pull Margie from this conversation.

"You go," Margie said. "I'm not quite done. I'll be there in a minute."

Trish looked from Margie to her mother and back again.

"It's okay, honey," Mrs. Clark said. "You can be excused. Thanks for offering to watch Tara."

Reluctantly, Trish got up from the table. She carried her dishes to the sink, rinsing them off. Finally she left the kitchen, afraid of what Margie might tell her mother.

"Margie, what's on your mind?" her mother asked, turning her full attention toward her older daughter.

Without looking up, Margie asked, "If I tell you something, will you promise not to tell?"

"You know I can't make that promise. But if it doesn't affect safety, your secret is pretty safe with me."

From her place outside the kitchen door, Trish heard Margie sigh before she began speaking. "I have a friend on the team whose parents don't know she's playing."

"Where do they think she goes when she's at practice?"

"Well, they know she's playing softball, but sometimes she comes to practice when she should be somewhere else."

"Where is she supposed to be?" her mother prodded.

"She has orchestra on Wednesday nights, but she would rather play softball."

"Why doesn't she talk to her parents about it?"

"She's tried, and they won't let her quit orchestra because they've spent so much money on it."

Her mother smiled. "I'm glad you know you can always talk to me about things like this. So back to your original question, would I let you quit—you need to understand the commitment you make to others. Yes, I would let you stop doing something, but probably not mid-season, in the case of softball, because others are counting on you. But art, that's an individual activity, and you could stop that if you chose to."

"But would you be mad at me?"

"No, honey, not mad." Her mother ran a hand under her daughter's chin gently. "You are a good artist, and I would like you to keep it up, but it's your decision."

"So you think Tr—I mean, my friend's parents should let her quit?"

"Every family is different. That's for them to decide. You asked me if I would let *you* quit. I obviously think she should tell her parents. Sneaking around can be dangerous. What if she got hurt? How would her parents know?"

Margie looked nervous. "You aren't going to tell, are you?"

She considered it. "No, for now I won't. I have a feeling this is a lesson she'll learn on her own."

From her spot outside the kitchen door, Trish leaned against the wall in relief.

"I know I said we wouldn't be playing games until August," Coach Kory told the girls after practice on Saturday, "but there was an opening for next weekend and I think it'll be good practice for us." He grinned broadly at them.

"We'll be playing at Kiwanis Park. Our first game is at 10:00. Meet there at 8:30 so we have time to warm up. We have three games on Saturday and the championship on Sunday. Pick up your uniforms from Mrs. Kerrington before you leave." He gestured toward his wife who sat in the bleachers and waved back.

"We'll only have ten girls because Ana has to go out of town. Are there any other conflicts I need to know about?" he waited and the girls all shook their heads.

"Let's bring it in and call it off," Coach Kory said, rallying the girls together in their traditional huddle.

After the girls finished their cheer, they went to pack up their equipment.

Sally asked Trish, "Are you going to be able to come next weekend?"

Trish smiled. "Sure. Weekends aren't a problem."

"But won't your parents wonder where you are all day?" Nikki asked. She and Margie had joined their discussion.

"I'll tell them I'm playing in a tournament. They won't think anything about it. They'll have to drop me off anyway. I can't ride my bike that far."

The relief showed on Margie's face. "I'm glad your parents will know where you are."

Trish knew Margie was thinking about the conversation Margie and Mrs. Clark had about Trish. It was nice that her friend was worried about her.

On Wednesday afternoon, Trish picked up her violin case and carried it to the kitchen. Her mother sat at the table, sorting through various magazines.

She looked up as Trish entered. "Did they move up the time for orchestra?" she asked.

"No, but I thought I'd go by Abby's house first, and her mom can give us both a ride."

"Okay. It's so helpful to have someone who lives so close in orchestra with you. Make sure to thank Mrs. Adams."

"Yes, ma'am," Trish replied. She kissed her mom's cheek and went out the backdoor.

She walked down the steps and out of sight of the kitchen window before she doubled back and entered the garage. There, she stashed her empty violin case behind a pile of boxes and picked up her softball bag. She knew the heat of the garage wouldn't be good for the violin, so she had hidden the instrument behind the clothes in her closet.

Moving quickly, she snuck back out of the garage and grabbed her bike from behind the building where she had placed it earlier in the day. She flung her pack onto her back and cut through the neighbor's backyard before pedaling back down to the sidewalk.

Chapter 9

Saturday morning, Trish's mom dropped her off at Kiwanis Park and drove away without even wishing her good luck. Trish had almost asked her to stay, but decided against it. There didn't seem to be much point. Her mother would never understand how much she loved softball.

The girls went through their usual warm-up routine. While they were jogging around the outfield fence, Trish noticed her mother's car was back in the parking lot and got a bad feeling. They finished their lap, and the girls headed to the dugout.

When they got closer, Trish saw her mom talking with Coach Kory. Her hands were gesturing wildly while Coach Kory's arms were crossed over his chest. He was looking at the ground intently, nodding along with her mother's comments.

Finally, they shook hands, and her mother stormed off back to the car. Coach Kory walked toward the dugout deep in thought. On the way, he stopped to talk to his wife who was sitting in the stands getting the scorebook ready for the game.

Mrs. Kerrington glanced at Trish quickly in response to a comment from the coach.

While Trish watched in horrified silence, Nikki and Sally joined her. "What's going on?" Sally asked.

"Nothing good," Trish answered with dread.

"Trish!" Coach Kory called and waved her over.

She met him behind the bleachers.

"Is there something you want to tell me?" Coach Kory asked.

She looked at her feet shamefully. She wasn't sure what her mother had said, but this couldn't be good. She decided to go with the most honest answer she could think of. "I just want to play softball."

The coach's face was red and she could tell he was very upset. "And you felt the only way to go about that was to lie?"

"My parents don't understand—"

"You forged your father's signature on the permission slip!" he snapped.

Trish was stunned. She had never heard Coach Kory raise his voice. She shook her head, "No, sir. I didn't. He signed those papers."

"But your mother said she didn't know you were practicing on Wednesday nights. She said you were supposed to be at orchestra rehearsal."

"He did sign them!" Trish emphasized. "He just didn't read them. He doesn't really care—"

He cut off her excuses again. "Trish, being part of this team is more than playing ball. We're like a family. And if you treat your real family like this—sneaking around, lying about where you are—how should I expect you to treat us?"

Trish had no words. Tears escaped her eyes before she could hold them back. "I didn't mean to hurt anyone," she said.

"You'll have to explain that to your mother."

She looked toward the parking lot for her mother's car, but it was gone. She turned back to Coach Kory confused.

"She's letting you stay for the day."

Trish couldn't believe her luck! Her heart raced, and a smile spread across her face.

"But you'll be sitting on the bench," Coach Kory finished. "I haven't decided what I'm going to do about this yet, but you can be assured I will not tolerate this behavior from anyone on the Tigers." With that, he walked away from her.

The light of hope Trish had was gone in an instant. She knew she was in big trouble—both here and at home. And she was going to have to suffer through this day thinking about what she had done wrong. She wiped her face and pulled herself together.

"Let's go, girls! The umpire is calling you all to the plate to go over the ground rules," Coach Dave said.

Trish joined her friends at the plate. Instead of focusing on what the umpire had to say, she knew from the strange looks they gave her that the other girls wanted to know what was going on. Margie slid up beside her and gave her arm a gentle squeeze of reassurance.

After the umpire flipped a coin to see which team would bat first, the Tigers went back to the dugout to get their equipment. They would be home team, and the other team would bat first. Coach Kory called out the lineup, and Trish's name wasn't on it.

Feeling shunned and humiliated, Trish sat on the bench and watched Sally warm up pitching.

"Batter, up!" the umpire called to get the game started.

Coach Sam glanced back at Trish from his place against the fence. "Get up here and cheer. Your team still needs you."

Trish did her best to shake off the deep sadness that continued to grow. She cheered as her team played their best and won 4-3.

"Great game!" Coach Kory said as the girls ran off the field after shaking hands at the end of the game. He gathered them all together to go over some highlights and make recommendations for improvements as they gulped down water.

"We're going with the same line-up next game. I'm going to move around the fielding positions a little and give others a chance to pitch."

The coach went on with his comments, but Trish's mind went numb. She wasn't going to play this game either! It was so hard to sit and watch as her team played without her. She wasn't sure if she could keep up the brave front.

"Take a break if you need it," Coach Dave said. "Be back here in 15 minutes to start the next game."

Most of the girls made a dash for the restrooms while others headed to the snack bar. Margie, Nikki, and Sally walked slowly with Trish to stand under the trees behind the backstop.

"So what's going on?" Nikki asked.

"I guess my mom figured out I skipped orchestra," Trish replied gloomily. "I'm in big trouble when my dad finds out."

"Why did she let you stay?" Margie asked. "No offense," she added quickly. "It's just my mom would have drug me out by my hair."

Trish shrugged. "I have no idea. I'm kind of surprised, too. Part of me wishes she would have. Sitting on the bench is more embarrassing by far."

"Someone has to be on the bench," Sally said soothingly. "You shouldn't feel bad about it. We'll all get our turn at some point."

"Yeah, but not as a punishment," Trish sulked. "Everyone knows something's up, and I'll bet they're talking about it in the bathroom."

"So?" Nikki said. "We're talking about it, too."

That got a small smile from Trish. "Thanks for trying to cheer me up. I know I screwed up. Now I just have to figure out what I'm going to do next. I won't be able to make practices on Wednesday nights anymore."

The three others exchanged glances. They hadn't thought of that.

"That sucks." Nikki stated what they were all thinking.

"Let's go!" the coaches called from the field to gather the team back together.

Trish and her friends jogged back to the dugout where Coach Kory gave his last-minute advice. Then the girls joined the other team at the plate for the umpire to go through the pre-game safety rules again.

After the second game, the girls came off the field downhearted. They had played hard but lost by one run.

"Tigers, lift up your heads. You played a great game," Coach Kory said. "You won't win every game, and we don't expect you to. We expect you to play your best. Did you play your best?" He took turns looking at the girls, but they were too discouraged to speak.

Trish felt even worse. She could only imagine how they were feeling, but she felt set apart because she wasn't able to contribute. She cleared her throat, "C'mon, Tigers! You did great!" It was a struggle, but she held her voice firm.

"Sal, you had 10 strike-outs. Emily, you made a great catch in right field." She went around the circle of friends she had made, trying to get each of them to smile. "They were older than we are and have been playing ball longer. Don't let this get you down. Remember, Sunday is for champions! These games don't count for anything but practice."

"She's right," Margie said. "Let's pull it together and win this next game so we get a good time slot for tomorrow. We want to be well rested for the championship game!"

"Bring it in," Coach Sam said, placing his right hand in the center of the circle.

Chapter 10

It was the bottom of the seventh inning, and the Tigers were up by one run. Trish still sat on the bench, ringing her hands. She was so nervous and felt helpless. The Tigers were in the field, and this was the last chance the other team had to bat. As long as they didn't score two runs, the Tigers would win this game.

Rachel was in center field, where Trish felt she would be under other circumstances. With no outs, the batter hit a short fly ball behind second base. Rachel initially took a step back, realized her mistake, and charged forward. As she ran to get under it, she misjudged the angle of the ball. In a full run with her glove out, her right foot came down on the ball as it hit the ground. With a cry of pain, Rachel's ankle went sideways and the ball shot off into right field. She hit the ground with a sickening thud. Amy, coming from right field, tried to react to the ball, but she was too close to stop it in time, and it flew past her into the grass.

The infield was yelling for the outfield to get the ball and throw it in. Amy chased it down and fired the ball hard to Margie, acting as cutoff at second base. But it was too late—the batter made it all the way to third.

Margie threw the ball to the pitcher as the coaches called time out and ran into center field. Rachel rolled in the grass holding her ankle with tears streaming down her face.

Girls on both teams went down on one knee as a sign of respect while the coaches checked out the injury. Finally, Coach Kory stood up, holding Rachel in his arms, and carried her off the field.

Trish grabbed her glove, prepared to fill in for Rachel in center field.

When Coach Kory was close enough to meet her eye, he shook his head no and nodded back to the bench. "Trish, grab an icepack." He placed Rachel on the bench.

Rachel's mom came in the dugout and helped get her daughter situated. Trish handed her a pack from the first-aid kit.

"Coach?" the umpire asked from behind the plate. "Are you entering a new player?"

"Nope." To the girls on the field he called out, "Left and right, squeeze toward the middle."

The girls complied, and the third baseman backed up a few steps to help cover the line for the left fielder.

The next ball was hit to the shortstop, who fielded it cleanly, throwing the girl out at first and not giving the runner on third a chance to advance.

"Coach, I understand what you're doing. I get it. But can I please help?" Trish begged quietly.

"Trish, actions have consequences. And sometimes those consequences affect more than just you." He clapped his hands together and directed encouragement to the field, "Okay, two more outs, girls. You can do it!"

Trish willed herself not to cry. She moved to the other end of the dugout and sat down on an upturned bucket. Her stomach was so upset she couldn't even cheer anymore.

The next batter swung late, driving the ball down the right field line. Amy had been playing closer to center field, leaving the path to the fence wide open.

She ran as fast as she could toward the ball as the girl who had been on third base crossed home plate. The batter had hit first base and rounded second base before Amy had a hand on the ball. The fence line was so long that Margie, playing second base, had to run deep into right field to accept the throw as a cutoff from Amy. She caught the ball, quickly turning, and threw the ball to Sally who stepped off the pitcher's mound to line up with home plate. She was ready to cut the throw and relay the ball if Margie couldn't make it all the way home.

By now, the batter had rounded third base and was running as hard as she could toward home plate. Sally caught the ball and spun with the momentum of her throw to zip the ball to Nikki behind the plate.

The ball slammed into Nikki's mitt, and she brought both her hands down for the tag. At the same time, the batter laid down on her left side, sliding toward the plate with her legs outstretched.

The dust cloud that was kicked up blocked the view for the spectators. "Safe!" the umpire yelled, waving his arms back and forth in front of his body.

The girls in the other dugout went wild, yelling and cheering. They clambered onto the field to congratulate their teammate for such a wonderful hit.

"Ballgame!" the umpire called.

Crestfallen, the Tigers headed toward home plate. Trish sat in the dugout in disbelief. Rachel cried harder from her place on the bench.

"Let's go," Coach Sam said, gesturing to Trish. "Get out there and shake hands."

The girls shook hands and returned to the dugout. Silently, they packed their gear and headed toward a spot under the trees where Coach Kory directed them. Dropping their bags, the girls slunk down to the ground, feeling miserable and disappointed.

Trish was the last to join them. She stood and kicked at the grass uncomfortably. "Before the coaches get here, I have something I want to say." She dropped her bag. "I'm really sorry. This is my fault."

Emily looked up from her place among the girls, "Why wouldn't he let you play?"

"I screwed up," Trish admitted. "I . . . I lied to my parents. I let them think I was going to orchestra when I was really sneaking out to come to practice on Wednesday nights."

Her teammates raised their eyes to look at her in surprise. She continued, "My parents wouldn't let me quit orchestra to play softball. But I love softball! All I wanted to do was play with you and get better, learning from you. You've been great friends. I'm sorry I let you all down. I wish I had found another way. I know what I did was wrong. Please forgive me."

Nikki reached up and grabbed Trish's hand, dragging her down. She tripped and fell on top of Sally, who laughed and shoved her into Margie. Margie rolled away and Emily leaned in to jab Trish playfully in the ribs. Before long, the girls were laughing and throwing gloves at one another. Someone pulled out a water bottle and dumped it over Trish's head. The girls squealed with laughter.

"Ahem," Coach Kory cleared his throat loudly. The girls straightened up and faced him. "Glad to see you're feeling better." He smiled.

"You all played a great game. I'm very proud of you—all of you," he said looking at Trish.

When the coaches had finished going over the learning points of the game, Coach Sam brought the girls together to call it off one more time.

"One, two, three, SOFTBALL!" they cheered in unison.

Trish flung her bag over her shoulder, turning to see her mother standing next to the tree. Trish hesitated a moment, then walked up to her. "I'm sorry, Mom. There's no excuse for what I did. It won't happen again."

Her mother looked at her sternly. "I should hope not," she replied.

Trish dropped her eyes.

"Those girls need you," her mother went on.

Trish's head snapped up and caught her mother's smile.

"Patricia, there is no excuse for lying or sneaking. I won't have any of that." She reached out and took Trish's hand. "But there's also no excuse for me not listening to what is really important to you." She pulled Trish into a quick hug then released her. "At least you aren't a filthy mess today," her mother teased her. Hand-in-hand they walked to the car.

Chapter 11

Trish was sure she wasn't out of the woods yet. She still hadn't faced her father. And she had a decision to make to give up either softball or violin. Although she had been fighting to get out of orchestra for months now, with the possibility within her reach, she was starting to doubt her decision. She did enjoy the violin, and it made her feel good to play.

"Dinner!" her father called.

Trish steeled herself against the stern lecture she was bound to get from her father and headed down the stairs.

In the kitchen, her mother handed her a dish of food to put on the table. They hadn't talked more about what happened since they got home. She could tell her mother was disappointed, but she didn't think she was mad anymore.

The three of them sat together at the table and began to dish out food.

"Patricia had three ball games today," her mother said conversationally to her husband.

"Really?" he said distractedly. "Please pass the potatoes."

Mrs. Murphy picked up the bowl. "I think we should go watch her games tomorrow," she suggested.

Trish was dumbstruck. This is the last thing she had expected.

"Tomorrow? I don't think so," Mr. Murphy answered, glancing at the television that was on in the next room. He reached for the bowl his wife was offering to him.

When she didn't release it, he turned to her, confused.

"The game starts at 9:00. I told the coach we would be there," her mother said with more firmness than Trish had ever heard before.

Her father glanced first at his wife, then Trish. "Okay, if you say so," he agreed.

Mrs. Murphy released the dish and smiled at Trish. "Honey, would you like more meat?"

Sunday morning Margie's mom pulled in to Trish's driveway to pick her up for the game. Trish hauled her gear to the van and piled in the backseat with Margie, the car seat with Margie's sister in between them.

"Good morning, Trish," Mrs. Clark said.

"Good morning, Mrs. Clark. Thanks again for the ride."

"Any time, dear," she replied, putting the car in gear.

"Well???" Margie asked in a hushed whisper.

"Well, what?" Trish answered innocently.

"You must not be grounded for life," Margie said. "So what did your parents say?"

Trish couldn't feign indifference any longer. She turned sideways in her seat to face her friend. "You aren't going to believe this! My parents are coming to the game!" she said excitedly.

"No way! That's great!" Margie said beaming.

Trish's mood changed in an instant. "I hope the coach lets me play."

"Me, too," Margie said. "Rachel's ankle is sprained, and she won't be able to play for a few weeks."

"Crap!" Trish said.

"Crap!" Margie's toddler sister repeated.

All three girls broke into giggles.

When the girls climbed out of the van at the field, Nikki and Sally rushed over to them. Sally gave Trish a quick hug, "Glad to see you in one piece," she said.

"Glad to be in one piece," Trish admitted. "I don't know what's going to happen after this weekend, but for now, I'm here. Mom didn't want the team to be a player short for the finals."

"That sure is good of her, all things considered," Nikki said.

The girls ran through their drills and went back to the dugout for water.

Rachel hobbled through the opening in the fence on her unwieldy crutches. The girls gathered around her in sympathy. "Nothing broken," she reported. "Just a bad sprain." She held up her foot to let them examine the thick bandage around it.

"Ladies," Coach Sam said.

The girls turned toward his voice and saw a new girl standing by his side, dressed in a Lady Tigers' uniform. Trish's heart sank.

"This is Jana. She has graciously agreed to play with us until Rachel heals."

The girls smiled and waved at her. Jana smiled meekly.

Trish swallowed the lump in her throat and approached Jana. "Want to play catch to warm up?" she asked.

"Thanks. That would be great." Jana dropped her bat bag and pulled out her glove. The two girls went behind the dugout to throw the ball.

"Players and coaches to the field!" the umpire called.

The girls from both teams took their place beside home plate to go over the safety rules again and wait for the umpire to flip the coin. While the umpire droned on, Trish's eyes swept the stands. At first she didn't see them. But then her mom's pink hat fluttered in the breeze and caught her eye. They were sitting in lawn chairs at the end of the bleachers. Her father was engaged in conversation with another father sitting to his left.

Trish broke out into a grin and nudged Margie who was standing beside her. Margie's eyes followed Trish's line of sight. Margie smiled too and elbowed Nikki.

Nikki glanced at her, then to where she was looking. She nodded, gesturing for Sally to look. The four girls shared a meaningful smile.

The umpire released them to their dugouts.

Coach Kory called them together in a circle. "Girls, let's start with the same line up we started with yesterday. Trish, are you ready?"

Trish glanced up, startled. "Yes, sir."

"You're going in for Rachel. Get your glove."

Chapter 12

Dirty, sweaty, and exhausted, Trish was the happiest she had been in years. The Lady Tigers stood in a semi-circle around the tournament director, receiving their second place trophies.

The girls were initially disappointed when they lost the championship game nine runs to eight, but the coaches were proud of them. This had only been their first tournament as a team, and they were playing in a level above their age bracket.

"Trish Murphy," Coach Kory called her name.

She stepped forward, shook his hand, and held the trophy high in the air for her parents to see. She could see them standing in the back of the crowd—in the back perhaps, but they were clapping. They were there!

After all the Tigers had been called, the girls clapped politely for the winning team as their coach called their names. Then they all headed back to the dugout to pack up their gear.

The girls sat in a disorganized gaggle under a shade tree away from the softball fields. One of the parents passed out cold drinks while they waited for the coaches to make their way over for the after-game chat.

Sally leaned back against her bat bag and placed a cool, wet towel over her face.

"You look much better that way," her sister teased.

Without looking up, Sally threw an empty water bottle at Nikki's voice.

"Hey!" Margie yelped.

Sally jumped up, "I'm so s—"

Margie laughed and tossed the bottle back at her.

Soon the girls were in a mini-war, tossing batting gloves, wet towels, and water at each other.

"Glad to see you're having so much fun," Coach Sam broke in.

"That's what sports are all about," Coach Dave added. "If you aren't having fun, it isn't worth your time."

"I want to thank Jana for joining us today. Luckily, we didn't have any other injuries, but it's always good to have a bench," Coach Kory said.

The girls smiled gratefully at Jana as the coach continued. "Now, let's talk about the future."

Trish hung her head, the wind going out of her. She knew that this was likely her last time with the team. Her mom was still pretty upset that Trish had lied and had not agreed to let Trish quit orchestra.

"We're running into a problem with our practice schedule." He addressed the parents that were standing in a loose circle around the girls. "Now that tournaments are starting, we won't be able to practice on the weekends very often. I'd like to go to two practices during the week."

Most parents were nodding their heads in understanding. Trish couldn't bring herself to see her parents' reaction.

"So I would like to switch to Tuesdays and Thursdays. If we don't have a tournament on the weekend, we'll try to get some time in Saturday morning."

Trish felt a sharp jab to her ribs. Reflexively, she looked toward the source. Margie was grinning ear-to-ear. Then the coach's words hit her. Tuesdays and Thursdays! Not Wednesdays! She wouldn't have to miss orchestra!

She didn't hear the rest of the coach's speech. She was practicing what she would say to convince her parents to let her stay with the Tigers.

When the coaches were done, Trish hefted her bag over her shoulder as she walked toward the parking lot.

Her father was talking to the third baseman's dad.

"I hope to see you at the next tournament," the man said, reaching out his hand to Mr. Murphy.

"I'll be there," Mr. Murphy answered with a big smile, taking his hand.

Trish couldn't believe her ears. She walked closer, and her father put his arm around her shoulders, giving her a squeeze. "Great game, Trish."

"Yes, Patricia, that was more interesting than I thought it would be," her mother said. "But will you please take off those filthy shoes before you get into the car?"

Trish glanced at her father, and he rolled his eyes. Trish burst into laughter. This certainly was a great day!

#######

Definitions

Fastpitch softball: The ball is pitched underhand with no arc, and typically with speed. The speed varies depending on the age, skill of the pitcher, and type of pitch thrown.

Change-up: A pitch that is thrown much slower than the fastpitch. It is meant to catch batters off guard and cause them to swing early and miss.

Infield: A dirt square with a base in each corner. The distance between bases changes depending on the age of the players. Sometimes baseball has grass on the infield for older players.

Outfield: The grassy area behind the infield that stops (usually) at a fence.

Field: The place where softball (or baseball) is played. Typically a dirt infield with a grassy outfield.

Diamond: This refers to the infield, plus the dirt around it all the way to the grass. Because the infield is positioned so the batter stands at one of its corners, it is called a diamond rather than a square.

Home plate: A five-sided, flat piece of rubber set level with the ground. The pitcher throws the ball toward the plate so the batter can hit it.

Rubber or Mound: The place where the pitcher stands to pitch the ball toward home plate.

Pitcher's circle: A circle drawn in a wide area around the pitcher's rubber.

Batter's box: A rectangle drawn on either side of the plate in chalk that is large enough for the batter to stand (right- or left-handed). The batter is allowed to stand anywhere within the box, but must be in the box when hitting the ball.

Umpire: The person that stands behind the catcher at home plate. The umpire calls balls and strikes, and ensures that everyone is following the rules of the game.

Runner: A batter that has made it to a base without getting out.

Lead off: In fastpitch softball, the runner cannot leave the base until the ball leaves the pitcher's hand. That gives them a slight head start when the ball is hit. Just because they take a lead, it does not mean they are required to run to the next base. But the runner can be tagged out if a fielder touches them with the ball when they are not touching the base.

Steal: If the runner chooses to run to the next base when the ball has not been hit, it is a steal. They take the risk of being tagged out so it doesn't happen every time.

Foul ball: A ball hit by the batter that does not stay within the boundaries drawn in chalk starting from home plate, straight over first base and out to the fence. Another line is drawn from home plate over third base and out to the fence. A "fair ball" must be inside those lines when it hits the ground.

Strikes: A ball pitched over the plate between the knees and armpits of the batter. It also refers to when a batter swings and misses the ball. A foul ball is also a strike.

Ball: In reference to balls and strikes, a ball is when the pitch is not over the plate, or is lower than the batter's knees, or is higher than the batter's armpits.

Strike out: A batter gets three strikes, and then she or he is out, and it's the next person's turn to bat. Foul balls are counted differently. In most cases, a foul ball on the third strike does not count, and the batter can continue to try until the ball is hit fair or a third strike is called.

Bunt: Instead of swinging at the pitch, the batter turns to face the pitcher and puts the bat across the plate. In this way, the ball hits the bat and doesn't travel as far, usually stopping somewhere between the catcher and the pitcher.

Fly ball: A ball hit into the air with an arc.

Line drive: A hard hit ball that has no arc.

Positions: The places on the field where the players stand. The exact location will change depending on the play, where the runners are on the field, and what the defense thinks the batter is going to do. In addition to the title of the position, the positions are also assigned position numbers that the scorekeeper uses to track the game. See the numbers next to the positions below.

1. **Pitcher**: The person that stands on the pitcher's mound and throws the ball over the plate. The pitcher's goal is to strike the batter out. For softball, the ball must be pitched underhand. For baseball, it is thrown overhand.

2. **Catcher**: The player that squats behind home plate to receive the pitch.

117

Because they are so close to the batter, the catcher must wear a helmet, mask, chest protector, and shin guards. Sometimes the catcher will also have a special glove that has extra padding. This is called a catcher's mitt.

3. **First baseman**: To the catcher's right, there is a bag (usually white) a certain distance down the foul line. The first baseman stands with the bag about four feet to her left.

4. **Second baseman**: Halfway between the first base bag and the second base bag. The second base bag is opposite home plate on the field.

5. **Third baseman**: To the catcher's left, there is a bag (usually white) a certain distance down the foul line. The third baseman stands with the bag about four feet to their right.

6. **Shortstop**: Halfway between the second base bag and the third base bag.

7. **Left field**: In the grass behind the shortstop.

8. **Center field**: In the grass behind the second base bag.

9. **Right field**: In the grass behind the second baseman.

Line-up: The order in which the batters hit. It can be in any order the coach decides, but the batters must remain in the same order throughout that game. A player can be replaced during a game, in which case the new batter must bat in the spot the person replaced was batting.

Out: Each team gets three outs per inning. An out can be made in many ways: striking out, tagging a base runner when she is not touching the base, catching a hit ball before it touches the ground, and throwing a hit ball to a base ahead of the runner when the runner is required to move. There are others, but this covers the most common examples.

Inning: When each team has had three outs the inning is over. The "top of the inning" is when the first team to bat is batting. The "bottom of the inning" is when the team that fielded first is batting. Softball is played for seven innings, unless there is a tie; then the game may go longer. Baseball typically plays nine innings.

Time limit: Often in tournament settings, a time limit is set on a game. It may be an hour and fifteen minutes or seven innings, whichever comes first. The time limit is set by the tournament director and can vary on different days or different tournaments. This helps keep the tournament on schedule.

Home team: The team that is in the field (defense) first at the beginning of the game.

Visitors: The team that bats (offensive) first at the beginning of the game.

Discussion Questions

1. Why do you think Trish lied to her parents?

2. What lesson did Trish learn?

3. What lesson do you think Trish's parents learned?

4. How could Trish have avoided her problem?

5. Is Trish a good friend or not? Please explain.

6. Who was your favorite character and why?

I hope you enjoyed reading about Trish and her friends. There is more to come and more players to meet. If you have ideas you want to share with me or softball questions to ask, please get in touch with me at BlueDragonPub@cox.net. I'd love to hear from you.

Watch for new Lady Tigers' books coming soon by Dawn Brotherton

Margie Makes a Difference

About the author

Dawn Brotherton is the author of five books, including the Jackie Austin Mystery Series and now the Lady Tigers Series. She is also a contributing author to *A-10s Over Kosovo,* a compilation of stories about being deployed for Operation ALLIED FORCE. Dawn has been awarded a Global Ebook Bronze Award for her writing. She is hard at work now on more Lady Tigers' adventures for young readers.

She is currently serving at the Pentagon in Washington, DC. as a colonel in the United States Air Force.

51020811R00072

Made in the USA
Charleston, SC
13 January 2016